AUTHOR
Townsend, J. David

TITLE
THE CATS STAND ACCUSED

The Cats Stand
Accused

J. David Townsend

The Cats Stand
Accused

Illustrated by Leonard Shortall

1 9 6 1

HOUGHTON MIFFLIN COMPANY BOSTON

The Riverside Press Cambridge

I

IN NEXT to the last week of summer vacation, the joys of the long hot days suddenly dwindled. It had been raining steadily since Monday, and the wind, still blowing cold from the northeast, held out little promise of better weather for the next few days. The children took this in bad part, looking on the rain as an enemy that had put a premature end to their pleasure. They complained that their last few days of freedom were being wasted.

There were so many things still to do — so many spots on the Island still to explore, so many games to be played out, so many wild crabapples and blackberries to be picked, so many fish to be caught. Now the tree house would probably not get finished before they went back to Boston, and they never would

1

know which was the better ball team. Rain, rain, rain! What a way for a vacation to end!

Mrs. Reed did her best to make the hours of confinement seem shorter. She had the boys keep a driftwood fire burning in the wide living-room fireplace. When one game had lost its appeal she proposed another, got the children about her and told stories of her childhood in Colorado; she offered a prize for the best cookies, and made a whopping plateful of stuffed nuts and dates. Still the boys were bored. They whispered to each other that it was easy for Mother and the girls to be happy indoors, as they were used to being cooped up. Boys needed fresh air and all outdoors to play in.

The living room, which had once been the kitchen of the old Reed house, was as attractive a place as any to be shut up in. Running across the entire length of the house behind the parlor and the dining room, it still had its original wide floor boards and a Dutch oven set in the thickness of the brick wall. High-backed couches framed the fireplace, and a huge blackened kettle swung from a crane over

2

the flaming logs. From the bare beams hung three ship models; and on the mantel was another full-rigged ship, imprisoned in a bottle since the days when proud whaling vessels sailed in and out of the harbor.

It was Friday afternoon. Harry and Paul, thirteen and nine respectively, had just finished a game of Scrabble. Mary and Jennie, twelve and seven, were down on the floor dressing paper dolls. Harry got up, stretched and walked over to the window. He was a big, strong-limbed boy, just entering the age when the voice wanders uncertainly between grumbles and squeaks. He shivered as he looked at the ocean beyond the jetty, leaden-gray and beaten flat by the pelting rain.

"Who'd believe we ever had fun rowing around on that?" he asked.

Paul had come over and stood by his side. "I don't believe it's ever going to stop raining," he grumbled.

"Oh, it'll stop all right as soon as we get back to Boston," Harry said. "That's the way weather always behaves."

"Yes, weather is awful contrary," Paul said.

3

"We ought not have let it know we needed these last two weeks so badly."

From down on the floor Mary called out, "Stop grumbling! Your words won't improve anything . . . Get something to do, like Jennie and me. The rain'll stop when it's good and ready."

The boys, still looking out of the window, saw someone wearing a slicker, all bent over against the driving rain, turn the corner of the house and disappear in the direction of the Van Pelt cottage.

"What in the world is anybody doing out in this storm?" Harry asked.

"Looks like a girl," Paul said.

At that moment Mother came into the room. "Where are the cats?" she asked, a sort of tragic note in her voice.

As if in answer to her question, a melancholy *meow*, accompanied by a vigorous scratching, was heard at the outside door. Paul opened it, and a pair of dripping cats, a mother and her half-grown kitten, sidled into the room.

4

"It's true then — what Lydia Van Pelt says!"
Mother cried.

"What about Lydia? What's she been saying now?" Mary asked.

"She just came over to tell me that one of
her guinea pigs is missing, and she accuses our
cats of eating it."

"So that was Lydia we saw going around the
corner," Paul said uninterestedly.

"Yes. She must have been terribly upset to come out in all this rain," said Mother.

"Huh! Lydia Van Pelt! What did she have to say?"

"What I told you. She said she went out to feed her guinea pigs a little while ago, and found one of them missing. And she claims that earlier in the afternoon her mother saw our cats on top of the cage, running their paws down through the wire."

Jennie had taken the kitten, George, on her lap and was drying his fur with her handkerchief. "I don't believe a word of it," she declared.

"Of course not," Harry added. "Those Van Pelts have never liked our cats. Lydia said the other day that Beatrice and George had better keep away from her guinea pigs if they knew what was good for them."

"Those ugly old guinea pigs!" Jennie cried.

"Still," said Mother, "you will admit it does look bad. The door of the cage *was* open and one guinea pig *was* gone; and our cats do hang around the Van Pelt yard. You know how many times we've had to call them home."

6

"I suppose cats *would* eat guinea pigs," Paul muttered.

"Just the kind of pets you'd expect Lydia and Alexandra Van Pelt to keep!" Mary said. "Cold and stupid, like them."

"Yes, ugly and dumb like them," Jennie added.

"Girls, girls," Mother said. "Be fair! Lydia and Alexandra probably love their pets as much as you love yours. Poor Lydia was crying so hard she could hardly speak when she was over here. I should feel very bad about it if it turned out that our cats had eaten the harmless little animal."

Beatrice, the mother cat, had finished licking the water out of her fur and had stretched out in complete satisfaction in front of the fire. "Poor Beatrice!" Paul said, pushing her gently with his foot. The cat opened one eye and gave a couple of licks to the spot the shoe had sullied, then went back to sleep again.

Beatrice was half Siamese. A rich gentleman from Bangkok, a business associate of Father's, had brought with him to Boston a female of the purest breed, given him, he

claimed, by the King of Thailand himself. A
brief friendship between the aristocratic female and a vulgar alley cat had resulted in five
mongrel kittens, of which Beatrice was one.
She was near-black, with only two marks of
royal birth about her — a kinked tail and a
rasping meow. Of Siamese there was nothing
at all in poor George.

"Well, what are we going to do about it?"
Harry asked.

"They don't expect us to kill our cats, I
hope," Mary said.

"I really don't know what to do," Mother
said thoughtfully. "We certainly can't close
our eyes to the whole business. We shall have

to keep the cats out of the Van Pelt yard, even if it means shutting them up in the cellar."

"Oh, Mother! Keep the poor things in the dark cellar just to please those people!"

"Remember, Beatrice and George may have eaten their pet. That's serious . . . I suggest we wait till Father gets here, and let him decide. You know Father is always just. Besides, he is very anxious to be on good terms with Mr. Van Pelt, whom he has to meet often at the club."

The Van Pelts, unlike the Reeds who had inherited their house from an aged aunt, were newcomers in Nantucket. This summer they were occupying the beautiful old Cushing house — one of the show places of the ancient whaling town — that they had restored and furnished at great expense. Back of the house lay a formal garden enclosed by a hollyhock-lined white fence. It was in this garden that the Van Pelt girls kept their guinea pigs.

Mrs. Reed had done her best to encourage friendship between her own and the neighbors' children; but it had not always been easy sailing. Mary and Jennie had often complained that Lydia was "snooty," that she thought herself better than the "natives." And as for the boys, they were reluctant to have anything at all to do with the Van Pelt girls.

Now Mother went on: "We don't want to do anything that would create hard feeling between our two families. It's true that there's only one more week left of the present season, but we shall all be coming back next summer. Imagine trying to live next door to people with whom you were always quarreling! Life wouldn't be possible . . . Now, let's not do or say anything about this guinea-pig business till Father gets here tomorrow afternoon. Is that a bargain?"

Everybody agreed that that would be the wisest line of conduct. The cats in the meantime were not to be allowed to go out, for fear that the sight of them in the Van Pelts' yard might throw even darker suspicion on them. Then Mother went back to her kitchen duties and the children returned to their games.

George had got down from Jennie's lap and had curled up beside his mother, one little paw flung around her neck. As they slept there

10

they looked so helpless and innocent that Mary cried out, "Imagine anybody thinking such a wicked thing about Beatrice and our little George!"

THE NEXT morning the wind had fallen and the rain had stopped, though the sky was still overcast. The radio promised complete clearing by noon, with warmer weather and sunshine.

This good news, with the prospect of being able to get outdoors again, brought the Reed family to the breakfast table in high spirits. The food tasted better than it had on' the stormy mornings, and a mountain of pancakes was consumed. The conversation naturally turned to the subject of the cats and the guinea pig. Mrs. Reed had a fresh bit of information to impart to the children.

"Last night," she said, "after you had all gone up to bed, I had a telephone call from Mrs. Van Pelt."

"About their old guinea pig, I bet," said Mary.

"Yes, about the guinea pig. She was very sweet, but I could feel that she was terribly upset. She seemed to be quite sure that the cats had eaten the girls' pet. She didn't say they *might* have done it; she came out plainly and said, 'Your cats were playing on the guinea-pig cage this afternoon, and they ate one of them — the male.'

"What could I say? I tried to be sweet, too, and told her how sorry we would be if that were the case. Then she asked how she was going to be sure that the cats would not eat the remaining guinea pig. Of course, I had to promise her we would keep the cats shut up till we were ready to go back to the city."

"Oh, Mother! How could you?"

"Now, what else could I say? . . . Before we hung up I told her we were expecting your father today and would put the matter in his hands. She said, in a tone of voice suggesting she had a mouthful of vinegar, that she hoped Mr. Reed would find some way to compensate them for the loss of such a valuable pet."

13

"Shucks! You can buy a guinea pig any-where for a dollar!"

"But these are extra-fine animals, it seems. Some sort of rare species."

"Anything belonging to the Van Pelts would be rare and expensive. Not like our plain old alley cats," said Paul.

"Alley cats!" Mary said. "Beatrice is half royal, and little George a quarter."

"By the way," Harry asked, "where are the cats now?"

"In the cellar," Mother said. "I put them down there last night, and I've been too busy this morning to get them up and feed them. Harry, will you see to them?"

Harry went to the cellar door and called, "Here Beatrice! Here George! Kitty, kitty, kitty! Here Beatrice! . . . That's funny, they don't answer."

"Oh, they're not down there any longer," Jennie said innocently. "They were crying at the door when I came downstairs, so I let them out."

"You let them out!" cried Mother. "Oh, good heavens!"

14

"I didn't know you wanted them kept in," Jennie said, sensing that something was wrong and beginning to cry.

"What will Mrs. Van Pelt think of me?" Mother said. "The miserable beasts are probably over in their yard at this very moment, clawing at the cage — if they haven't already eaten the remaining guinea pig. I'll never be able to look Mrs. Van Pelt in the face again!"

"Please Mother," said Mary. "Don't get all worked up. I'll go and see what they're doing."

She had scarcely stepped over the doorsill when she was back in the room again. "Come here, quick!" she cried.

Everybody dashed out; and there, in an angle of the porch, were Beatrice and George, with swollen tails and fur standing up along their backs, tearing at a *small black-and-white animal!*

"Just as I feared!" shrieked Mother. "The other guinea pig!"

Harry kicked the spitting cats aside and picked up the victim. "It's just a skin. There's nothing in it!" he said.

15

Mary ran over to the fence and peered into the Van Pelt garden. "It isn't the second guinea pig, at least," she shouted. "She's still in the cage."

"That's something to be thankful for," Mother said with a sigh of relief.

Harry held the skin in his hand as gingerly as if it were burning him. "We'd better not be seen with this skin," he said. "Let's get rid of it right away. If Lydia saw us now, nothing could convince her our cats didn't do it." And without further thought he threw the incriminating evidence into a tangle of wild-rose bushes growing on the rock-strewn vacant lot back of the Reed house.

Lydia and Alexandra had come out into their garden and were standing by the guinea-pig cage talking soberly, without once looking in the direction of the Reeds. "We'd better get into the house," Mother said, "if we don't want to arouse their suspicion. And, for heaven's sake, take the cats in with you."

As it was still chilly, the boys built a fire in the living-room fireplace, while the girls helped Mother clear away the breakfast things.

16

Afterward the children gathered around the fire to discuss the situation.

"Let's have an inquest," Harry suggested. "And examine all the evidence we have, both for and against."

"Like in a detective story," said Mary.

"Something like that. But we shall need Mother . . . Mother, Mother, can you come here, please?"

Mother came in with a pile of linen in her arms. "I suppose it's about that miserable guinea pig," she said. "Aren't you going to let me get anything else done today?"

"Not till this matter is cleared up," Harry answered grimly. "This is the most important thing that has happened all summer . . . Now, where does the evidence point?" Harry had watched a good many TV trial shows and was familiar with their specific vocabulary.

"If you ask me," Paul said, "it looks as if Beatrice and George really ate that guinea pig."

"I wouldn't want the Van Pelts to hear me say it, but I agree with Paul," Mary said.

"Me, too," said Jennie.

17

And Mother said, "That's the way it looks to me."

"Hum. Looks pretty bad for the cats," said Harry. "But let's not be too quick to come to a conclusion . . . Paul, get me a sheet of ruled paper — and a pencil. Now, I'm going to make two columns, one labeled *for,* the other *against,* and set down under those headings all the scraps of evidence we have. All right . . . Now, Mary, what makes you think the cats are guilty?"

Mary thought a minute before answering. "Well, they were seen on the cage just before the animal disappeared."

"That's the strongest piece of evidence," Mother said.

Harry wrote this under the heading *against* as Number One: *Cats were seen near the cage minutes before the crime.*

"Now, what next?"

"The cats had the skin this morning," Paul said slowly. Harry gave this Number Two and wrote, *Cats were found tearing the guinea-pig skin.*

Then Jennie said, "The cats were out in the

rain yesterday, and the door of the cage was open, and the guinea pig was gone."

"Yes, we have those facts already. Is there anything else?"

"Isn't that enough?" Mother asked. "Added to the fact that our cats will eat anything that runs on four legs, from mice to rabbits."

"I'll put that in for good measure." And Harry wrote, *Cats have a natural liking for animals and will eat guinea pigs.*

"I have to admit it looks pretty bad for the defendants. But now let's ask a few questions . . . First, did anybody *see* George and his mother eat the guinea pig?"

"Of course not," Mother said. "If they had, we shouldn't be holding this inquest. But remember, we did see them tearing the skin."

"But the skin was empty."

"That doesn't prove anything. They had already eaten the body."

"Wait a minute!" Mary cried. "How could the cats have eaten the body — flesh and bones — without eating at least a part of the skin?"

"A wonderful question!" shouted Harry. "That gives me an idea." He laid down his pencil and jumped to his feet. "Come on, let's go out and find that skin! I think everything depends on the condition it's in."

They all rushed over to the vacant lot, and after a quarter of an hour's search, came back in with muddy feet and scratched hands, Harry carrying the skin at arm's length.

"Oh, it's all wet!" cried Jennie, holding her nose. "And it stinks!"

The bit of fur was indeed an unpleasant-looking object. Harry laid it down on an old newspaper, and overcoming his distaste, spread it out flat so that it could be examined.

"The first thing to settle is, *do we recognize this fur?*"

"Naturally," Paul said. "It's the Van Pelts' black-and-white guinea pig. I'd know that anywhere."

"Are you sure of that beyond the shadow of a doubt?" Harry asked, airing his detective-story vocabulary.

Everybody was sure: they swore to it. Therefore Harry said it should be preserved and marked *Exhibit 1* for the defense.

"It could serve just as well for the prosecution," Mother suggested.

"It might, but I could break that down," Harry said. "Now Mother, I ask you to examine this exhibit carefully . . . You don't have to touch it with your hands. Spread it out with these pencils . . . Does it look to you as if it had been chewed or partly eaten?"

"Why, no! Oh, I see what you're driving at, Harry. This skin looks as if it had been slit open — down the belly — as with a sharp knife. Cats never could have done such a clean job."

"Then, after a careful examination of this piece of evidence, you would say it was not likely the victim met death at the hands — or teeth — of cats?"

"I certainly would."

"Now I will ask the other witnesses to examine the skin and give their opinion." One after another, Mary, Paul, and Jennie looked the skin over. They agreed with Mother that there was no sign of the skin having been torn or chewed by the teeth of a cat or any other animal. It looked more like the work of a human being with a knife.

"All right," Harry said. "That being established, we will set it down on the *for* side of our sheet . . . You see, things don't look quite so black now . . . And another question: who fed the cats last evening?"

"I did," Mary said. "Why do you want to know?"

"Oh I had another hunch . . . Did they seem hungry? Did they eat all their food?"

"They were starved, and gobbled up their chowder so fast I had to get them some more."

"Aha! Now I ask you: if those cats had just eaten a whole guinea pig, *would they have been hungry for their supper?*"

As the importance of this question dawned on them, everybody shouted at once, "Of course not!" Mary kissed her big brother on the cheek, Jennie threw her arms about him, Paul shook his hand manfully, and Mother said, "I'm proud of our young detective. Thanks to him, we now have reason to hope for the innocence of our poor cats. For a while it looked pretty bad for them."

Harry was flushed with satisfaction as he resumed the questioning. "There's still another point to clear up. Did the cats eat their breakfast this morning?" Mary said they had polished their plates.

"And when were they fed — before or after we found them with the skin?"

"After," said Mother.

"Then that proves that they could not have eaten the animal in the morning, after being let out of the cellar. Now you understand how important his piece of evidence is to the defense. We must keep the skin in the deep-freeze so it won't smell too bad when Father examines it."

Mother objected to that. She said the thing smelled so vile now that it would probably spoil every bit of food in the freezer, but Mary overrode her objection by promising to put it in an airtight container.

"And write on the jar *Exhibit 1*," Harry ordered. Then in a solemn voice, "I declare this inquest adjourned . . . Now, everybody get out and collect more evidence. Scour the neighborhood, and question everybody you meet. Only, be sure you don't let anybody suspect what you're up to."

"Let me be a Private Eye!" cried Paul. "Can I, Harry? Can I be a Private Eye?"

"You'll be Private Eye Number 1. But you all must go snooping. On second thought, Jennie had better stay with Mother. You can never be sure what she's going to say. And see that the cats don't get out again and make the business worse than it is. I'm going to beard the lion in its den, that is, go over and talk to Lydia Van Pelt. By the time Father gets here this afternoon the case must be pretty well solved . . . See you all at lunch."

3

Not caring to knock at the Van Pelt front door and go through the ordeal of polite greetings, Harry waited till Lydia and her little sister Alexandra came out into the garden before he went to "beard the lion in its den." In the meantime he changed his shirt and brushed his hair carefully, for he, like all the *natives,* felt a bit intimidated by the elegance of those two sisters.

There was no denying that they were truly lovely girls, almost fragile-looking with their golden hair, blue eyes, and delicate skin. They were constantly being warned by their loving "Mam-*ma*" to keep out of the sun, hold their heads up, and speak in low tones. This morning they looked like pictures, in freshly starched white dresses, standing amidst a mass of flaming early-autumn flowers.

Harry greeted them with a casual "Hello, Lydia; hello, Alexandra. I guess it's going to be a nice day."

Lydia's greeting was on the chilly side. Still, girls are girls; and Harry, in spite of his "roughness," was an unusually good-looking boy. In his place, Mary or any other girl would not have got a word out of Lydia, but Harry managed to make her talk.

After an exchange of commonplace remarks about the weather, the garden, and so forth, Harry came to the point.

"What's this I hear, Lydia, about your guinea pig?"

Lydia stiffened, Alexandra's pretty little face puckered, and she went and stood against the despoiled cage. "Your cats ate the husband yesterday — and just when the wife is going to have little ones."

"Too bad. But how do you know our cats did it?"

"You know we've told you a hundred times

27

to keep them out of our garden, for as soon as they get over here they jump on the cage and try to get my poor dears. I knew they'd get at them some day. Now one of them is gone, and who else but your dreadful cats could have taken it? Especially since Mam-*ma* saw them around the cage yesterday afternoon?"

"When we went out to feed them the door was open, and one of them was gone," sobbed Alexandra.

"They were not ordinary guinea pigs," Lydia said. "Pa-*pa* bought them from an exporter."

"We're awfully sorry," Harry said. "But we aren't convinced that our cats are responsible." On the last syllable of that long word Harry's voice, which had been going along nicely on a manly bass, suddenly jumped to a girlish soprano. He coughed and cleared his throat, blushing miserably.

"It's natural for you to want to defend your pets," Lydia said. "But we *know* they ate the poor thing. Imagine the way it must have suffered!" Lydia's blue eyes overflowed with sympathetic tears.

"May I take a look at the cage?" Harry asked, feeling like a brute in the presence of so much grief.

"Nobody can keep you from looking at it, but you'll not find anything to clear your cats."

Harry, glad to escape from the accusing eyes of the two girls for a minute, went and stooped down in front of the cage. It was made of strong wire with a cement floor, and seemed proof against thieving animals. The door had stout hinges and was kept shut by a hasp through which was run a thick wooden peg hanging at the end of a leather thong. It was this fastening that held Harry's attention. "See here, Lydia," he called. "No cat could have opened this door."

"Couldn't it?" Lydia replied, coming over to the cage. "I've seen cats open doors, and so have you. There isn't a lock they can't work open, if you give them time enough."

Harry did not try to answer this, but asked another question instead. "Are you absolutely sure the cage door was closed? Couldn't it have been left unlocked, so the guinea pig just pushed it open and wandered off?"

29

"Oh, no! I was the last one to give them food, and I *know* I locked the door."

"Well, then, could anybody from the outside have got to the cage yesterday afternoon without being seen?"

"Why, yes, I suppose so."

"Your mother saw the cats; she didn't see anybody else, but that doesn't mean that someone *didn't* touch the cage."

"I suppose somebody could have come into the garden. But nobody did. Who would take a guinea pig? People don't eat them."

"Possibly; but I have a feeling it was a human hand and not a cat's paw that opened that door . . . Well, Lydia, you can be sure we'll do all we can to make up for your loss — and we'll punish the cats. In the meantime we're keeping Beatrice and George shut up."

"It's too late now!" Lydia wailed. "Our dear pet is dead!" and a fresh torrent of tears rolled down her cheeks. Harry said goodbye and hurried home. There he took out his "evidence sheet" and under the heading *for* wrote a third item: *A cat could not open the guinea-pig cage door.*

31

Meanwhile Mary, Paul, and Jennie were looking for information elsewhere. Paul had an idea that it was possible the guinea pig had not been eaten at all, but had slipped out of the cage and was hiding somewhere.

"You're crazy," Mary said. "Didn't we find the skin?"

"Maybe he's running around without his skin," Jennie said.

"Yes, we found a skin; but it might be another animal's skin," Paul protested. "Almost all guinea pigs are black and white. It could be we've made a mistake."

"Of course, everything's possible," Mary admitted. "But it would be a terrible coincidence."

Still, after a short argument Mary agreed that they should look for the animal, limiting the field of their search to the immediate neighborhood since it was not likely that a guinea pig would wander far off. So they separated, each one taking one of the streets surrounding the Van Pelt house. They peered into gardens, poked among the weeds growing along the fences, crawled into hedges and clumps of bushes. Then together they beat every square foot of the vacant lot. Jennie, disregarding Harry's order, had come along with a handful of lettuce leaves which she waved invitingly in every nook and cranny. They asked everybody they met whether they had come across a guinea pig, but nobody had seen hide or hair of the missing animal.

Worn out, the three investigators sat down on the curb to rest and plan their next move. "We've proved to our satisfaction that the miserable beast isn't running around here," Mary said. "Now we must look for the killer."

"Where are we going to look for him?" Paul asked dejectedly.

"Well, we can't look for him unless we have some clue to lead us."

"And what clue have we got?"

"None at all, so far. But we can narrow down our search by asking and answering a few questions. First, who would want to kill one of the Van Pelts' guinea pigs? . . . Have they got any enemies in Nantucket? . . . What man or woman would hate them enough to want to do this terrible thing to them?"

As quick as a shot came back the answer, and from the most unexpected quarter. "Jake Salt," said Jennie.

"Poor Jake Salt!" said Mary. "Because he's ugly and funny and dirty, you want to blame everything on him."

"Wait a minute, Mary," cried Paul. "Little old Jennie may have something there! You ask who hates the Van Pelts. Well, Jake Salt certainly does. I saw him spit on the ground behind Mrs. Van Pelt's back when she passed him the other day."

"And he poured a tub of washwater into the gutter so it ran all over her feet, just as she was going by his house," shouted Jennie.

Jake Salt was a "character," in the language of Nantucket. He lived by himself in a tumble-down unpainted shack on the alley running along the far side of the vacant lot, and earned a poor living by selling worms and other bait to the summer fishermen. Because of his black hair and swarthy skin, he was credited with having Portuguese blood, perhaps even Indian blood in his veins. In the early part of the season he had been called in

34

by Mrs. Van Pelt to help the decorators by steaming the old paper off her walls. In the middle of the second day he had thrown down his tools and gone home, swearing he would never return. And he didn't, not even to collect the pay that was due him.

"Lydia told him he had fleas," Paul said.

"And the poor old man overheard Mrs. Van Pelt tell her cook, after he had been in the kitchen, to open the windows and let the bad smell out," Mary added.

"And after they said he had fleas, he came and shook his old pants over the fence just when Mrs. Van Pelt was having tea in the garden with some of her rich friends."

Mary summed it up: "Oh, he hates the Van Pelts all right, and had a motive for killing their guinea pig. Is that a clue?"

"It certainly is," shouted Paul, jumping to his feet. "I say we ought to go over and talk to Jake Salt right away!"

The young investigators found the old man sitting out in front of his house in a broken-down wicker rocker. He was indeed funny-looking, wizened and dirty, but the pair of

black eyes that glowed in his tanned face warned you that here was someone you had better not try to deceive.

Nobody found anything to say for an awkward minute, the three young people staring half frightened at the old man, and he staring coolly back at them. Jennie was hiding behind Mary, just sticking her head out far enough to see and be seen.

"Well, young'uns," Jake Salt drawled finally, removing his pipe from his mouth. "What kin I do fer you?"

"Oh, we just stopped by to say how-do-you-do," Mary said.

"And to ask you if it's going to clear up today," Paul added. This was a good opening, for Mr. Salt was proud of his ability to forecast the weather. He studied the sky a minute before answering. "Ay-eh. By two o'clock the sun'll be shinin' hot. We ain't goin' to have no more rain for some time."

"Oh, thank you kindly, Mr. Salt," Mary said. "Father's coming out by the two-thirty boat, and we want to go down to the pier to meet him."

"Wa-al, you kin go without fear o' gettin' wet."

Then Jennie came out from behind her older sister and had her say. "You haven't seen a guinea pig wandering around as if it was lost, have you, Mr. Salt?"

It seemed to Mary that the old man stiffened a little at the question, and his eyes looked more than ever like black beads. "Ain't seen no guinea pig," he said. "Whose guinea pig was it?"

"The Van Pelt girls'," Paul told him. "It disappeared yesterday afternoon, and they're blaming it on our cats."

"Them girls!" Salt muttered, his words heavy with scorn. "I don't think much o' them, nor their darned old guinea pigs."

"Do people eat guinea pigs, Mr. Salt?" Jennie asked innocently.

Again the old man stiffened. He puffed vigorously on his pipe, as if he had not heard the question.

"Don't be silly, Jennie," Mary said. "Of course people don't eat guinea pigs. They're to play with, or to study in hospitals and places."

"They can be et," Mr. Salt volunteered.

"Did you ever taste one?" Paul asked.

"Once . . . Tastes a little like rabbit . . . Pretty good eatin'."

"But I guess it's been a long time since you ate a guinea pig," Mary said.

"Nigh on fifty years . . . Wa-al, I got to go

down to the store, so you young'uns best be runnin' along."

The children said goodbye politely and walked off. But as soon as they were out of the old man's sight they began hugging each other and talking excitedly. "We're on the right track! Jake Salt's guilty . . . Did you notice how he looked when Jennie first mentioned the guinea pig? . . . He does eat guinea pig, and likes it . . . He had a motive for killing it . . . Wait till Harry hears about this!"

"Listen, all of you," Mary said as they walked into their own dooryard. "So far we haven't any real proof, but I think we can find stronger evidence . . . The messy old man doesn't put his garbage out, like everybody else, but throws his scraps and trash out back of the house. Now, if he did eat the guinea pig, he had to get rid of the bones, didn't he? And where did he put them? We know, don't we? . . . Now, Paul, while he's downtown you go over and see what you can find back of his house. If you find just one bone, one weeny-teeny guinea-pig bone, that'll be all the proof

39

we need." Having settled the matter, the junior investigators went into the house to report to their chief.

That afternoon the Van Pelt girls had a funeral for their lost pet. Lydia wondered whether it would be right to have a funeral without anything to bury. She asked their old cook about it.

"Mrs. Conners, do people ever give a person a funeral when they can't find the body?"

"Good land yes, dearie!" the cook replied. "Especially out here on the Island. Go through the old cemetery and read the men's names on the tombstones. Most of them were lost at sea in whaling days, but they had decent funerals just the same. I guess there are a lot of empty graves out here."

"Then it would be all right for Alexandra and me to have a funeral for our guinea pig that nasty cat ate."

"Of course it would. Besides, you don't have a funeral for the body; you have it for the soul." Mrs. Conners was a believing Christian.

"But do guinea pigs have souls?"

"Everything we love has a soul," the old woman said.

So, relieved of their doubt, the girls went ahead with plans for the funeral. Mrs. Conners helped them by lending them some of her old black dresses, of which she had a great number, as she rarely wore any other color than black. Lydia and Alexandra made themselves long veils out of an old black chiffon dress that their mother gave them. Their doll carriage was decently draped in crape to serve as a hearse.

Feeling that a funeral would not be complete without a procession of mourners, the girls recruited a half-dozen other children: a playmate of Lydia's from down the street, the cook's two grandsons, the gardener's boy, and the two little daughters of Millie, the upstairs maid.

Shortly after lunch the funeral procession left the Van Pelt house and headed toward the cemetery. First came the doll-carriage pushed by the gardener's boy, whose only mourning garb was an old yachting cap belonging to Mr.

41

Van Pelt. The carriage was empty, of course, but so draped as to hide that fact. Back of the hearse walked Lydia and Alexandra, unrecognizable under their black veils, tottering along on high heels and wearing long black gloves.

Then followed Lydia's friend in a black hat with plumes and a black dress that swept the street; then the two little girls, then the two boys, one a mere toddler who fell down and had to be set on his feet every few minutes. Spaced a good distance apart, they made an impressive procession.

As they came abreast of the Reed house, Lydia and Alexandra began to cry. "Oh dear, oh dear!" they wailed. "Our poor little guinea pig! Our poor darling! Oh, those awful cats!" The noise brought all the Reeds to the windows. For the benefit of the spectators the girls sobbed and wailed louder than before, and all the other mourners joined in. Down the street they went, leaving a trail of lamentations behind them.

In a quarter of an hour they went by again, this time headed toward home. While they were at the cemetery the Reed children had consulted together as to how they should take this performance. Paul was for throwing stones at them; Jennie wanted to stick out her tongue at them; Mary and Harry thought it best to do or say nothing.

"Don't you see they want us to make a fuss," Mary said, "and will be disappointed when we don't? Let's pretend we don't see them."

So they got away from the windows and stopped their ears, as the mourners, walking very, very slowly, raised their voices in a concert of moans and shrieks. Then the procession disappeared into the Van Pelts' front door.

4

Jᴀᴋᴇ Sᴀʟᴛ might have felt well pleased with his prophecy; for the sky did clear, and by half past two, when the family was to start down to the pier to meet Father, the sun was shining and the wind had veered to the south.

Beatrice and George, sensing that the weather had cleared, knowing there would be birds in the trees and little beasts abroad in the grass, begged to be let out. They tried the screens in one window after another and scratched at all the doors, then walked around mewing unhappily and rubbing themselves against chairlegs and people as they passed.

Once Mother caught Jennie moving furtively toward the front door with the two animals after her. "No, no, Jennie!" Mother called. "We mustn't weaken. Those cats must

44

not go out until this business has been cleared up . . . Put them down cellar now, so there will be no danger of their slipping outdoors with one of us."

Jennie obeyed with a heavy heart. The cats objected to being put in the damp cellar, away from light and heat and the company of people. Beatrice had to be pushed down the stairs, and George clung to Jennie's shoulder so stubbornly that his claws brought out tiny drops of blood under her blouse. Even after the family had rounded the house and got well on their way, they could hear pathetic howls coming from the open cellar window.

Main Street falls away sharply from the hill where the Reeds lived, down to the miniature harbor. From the top of the street that Saturday afternoon the sea, flooded with August sunlight, looked like a dark blue cloth on which a million diamonds were spread out for sale. Every once in a while, as a puffy white cloud drifted across the sun, the glitter faded, but only for an instant. Off on the horizon a smudge of black smoke marked the position of the incoming boat.

45

The children were utterly happy. Their joy defied analysis. The blue sky, the diamond-flashing sea, the warm air, the whaling captains' noble mansions along the street — all were a part of it. Not a stick or a stone or a breath could have been taken away without altering the perfection of the moment. So it was that the children danced down to the harbor, making it hard for Mrs. Reed to keep up with them, her heart and feet being a little heavier than theirs.

The boat took shape quickly, and within a quarter of an hour after the Reeds had got down to the port it was edging up to the pier. This was the high moment of the week. Seeing Father off on the boat Monday morning was wonderful, but meeting him on Saturday was even more wonderful. There was something dramatic about the way the great ship — it was colossal compared to the other craft in the harbor — bumped against the pilings of the pier with a wrenching and creaking and shivering, and the way the gangplank was run down and the first passenger stepped out on it. All their hearts beat rapidly — Mother's perhaps fastest of all — as Father, loaded down with boxes and bags, came into sight.

"Father, Father!" they all shouted, waving their arms and jumping up and down as if he were coming home after a year's stay in Timbuktu. Of course it was Mother he took in his arms first, then Jennie, then Mary, then Paul. He and Harry just shook hands. "Hello, Dad," Harry said in his new man's voice. "You're looking fine."

The children liked to wait around till all the passengers had debarked. The Saturday boat was generally crowded, but the threat of bad weather had discouraged the tourists, and only the regulars had crossed to the Island today. In a few minutes they had come off the boat and scattered, leaving the pier to the Reeds.

Harry picked up the heaviest suitcase, declaring, when Mary remonstrated, that his arms were quite as strong as Father's; and Father let him believe it. Everybody carried something so that Father had his right arm free to throw around Mother's waist.

"What a wonderful day it is!" he said, taking

a deep breath of the salty air. "And how good it is to get away from the city!"

"You're going to have a whole week to get rested," Mother told him.

Father smiled. "Get rested, huh? With all the packing to do and the place to be tidied up for the winter? . . . No, forget I said that. Of course I shall get rested, and we're going to have a great time together."

Then Jennie, clinging to Father's sleeve, suddenly burst out, "Daddy, Beatrice and George killed one of the Van Pelts' guinea pigs, and Lydia is mad, and the cats are shut up in the cellar, and . . ."

"Jennie!" Mother said sharply. "You know I asked you not to say a word about that business till Father had had a chance to change his clothes and catch his breath."

"She would blab it out!" Paul said.

"What's this about guinea pigs?" Father asked.

Jennie started to answer, but Mary put her hand over her mouth and pulled her back with her. "It's nothing," Mother said. "At least, nothing that can't wait. After supper

48

you'll hear the whole story. In the meantime, there are nicer things to talk about." And Mother began asking Father about people they knew in Boston.

While Father changed into his oldest, most comfortable clothes, the ladies of the family got an early supper ready. It was to be a feast, with clam chowder, baked lobster and blackberry dumplings. Father asked where the cats were, and was surprised to hear they were shut up in the cellar. "Ask no questions," Mother advised him, "and by and by you'll hear all about their doings."

The cats were very fond of Father, and as soon as they were let out they jumped on his lap. George washed his arm, and Beatrice tried to lick his face, both of them purring so loud they fairly made his body tremble. "My poor babies!" Father said, stroking one with each hand. "What have they been doing to you while I've been away?" Of course the cats told him nothing, but Jennie, who had squeezed affectionately under his arm, began, "You don't believe Beatrice would do anything wicked, do you?"

"Jennie, Jennie!" Mother warned.

At that moment Paul called, "Come and get it!" and they all sat down at the table. After supper they carried their favorite chairs or cushions out on the terrace and made a circle around Mr. Reed, everybody bursting with impatience to get to the business of the guinea pig. It was Mother who told the story — just the simple facts, without commenting on the guilt or innocence of the cats.

"Well, Father, how does it look to you?" Harry asked when she had finished.

"My boy, it looks to me — it looks to me as if our beloved cats had eaten the poor animal," Father said.

"Then how are you going to punish them?" Jennie asked.

"Aha, that's a hard question. Maybe we'll have to skin them, the way they skinned the guinea pig." There was a twinkle in Father's eye which took away a little of the awfulness of his answer. "Seriously though, kids, this is no laughing matter. We've always tried to be on good terms with our neighbors, and it would be too bad if a silly thing like this were

51

to create hard feelings. Personally, I have never believed parents should take part in their children's quarrels. I hope Mr. and Mrs. Van Pelt stay out of this, as I intend to do."

"But you must help us this time, Dad!" Harry cried.

"You see, we believe the cats aren't guilty," Mary said. "And we're getting evidence to prove it."

"Now, that sounds businesslike," Father said. "Have you got any favorable evidence?"

Then they all started talking at once, reporting what they had found out — the solid lock on the cage, the untorn condition of the skin, the cats' hearty appetites the evening of the crime, and the interview with Jake Salt. Exhibit 1 was produced, but was found to be frozen so stiff it could not be examined. Father was impressed, and said he would take Harry's word for it's not being mutilated. About Jake Salt he was skeptical.

"You kids mustn't jump at conclusions. You can't find the poor old man guilty on mere circumstantial evidence. That wouldn't be fair . . . In any case, you've done the right thing in keeping the cats shut up. We'll be going back to Boston in a week, and the whole thing will be forgotten before we come back next summer."

"But, Father," Mary said. "We must clear them now. Lydia will never, never forget it, and she'll get even with the cats in some way if she goes on believing them guilty."

"Well, how can we clear the cats? Wouldn't Lydia go on believing them guilty even if you got proof to the contrary?"

It was then the idea came to Harry. *"We'll have a trial!"* he said.

"Yes, we'll try them for murder in the first degree," Paul said, "and hang them if they're found guilty."

"Wait a minute," Mary objected. "If you're going to kill them, I won't have any part in it."

"We wouldn't hang them both — only Beatrice. George is a minor," Paul said.

"They wouldn't necessarily have to be killed," Mother said. "But if they're guilty, they'll have to be kept in prison till we go away. I like the idea of a trial."

Father, too, approved of the idea. In fact,

he got quite enthusiastic about it. He even offered to be Prosecuting Attorney. "For," he said, "I honestly believe the two cats ate the guinea pig. We've seen them eat all sort of animals — mice, moles, rabbits, even a wood-chuck. I'll do my best to hang them. It's up to you, if you wish them spared. An honest trial ought to satisfy Lydia Van Pelt."

"Then I'll be Attorney for the Defense," Harry said. "I'm sure they're innocent."

Then plans for a trial went ahead swim-mingly. Everybody agreed Father and Harry should be the two attorneys. Mother was to be Clerk of the Court. Mary, Paul, and Jennie would be witnesses. Father said the Clerk would first have to serve the witnesses with subpoenas.

"We'd have to subpoena Lydia and Alex-andra and Jake Salt, or it would be one-sided," Mary said.

Father agreed that Lydia, and perhaps Alexandra, should be brought in to testify. In fact, they would be his star witnesses. But he objected to calling Jake Salt. "His name must not be mentioned in this business," he said.

"There's already too much hard feeling between him and the Van Pelts."

"But I wanted him as my witness," Harry said.

"Well, maybe we could accept his testimony without his appearing in court. But his name must not be mentioned. Now, what date shall we set for the trial?"

"Monday afternoon, at the latest," Mary suggested. "The poor beasts will have to be kept in prison till the trial, so let's get it over as soon as possible."

They all laughed when Paul asked if the accused could not be let out *on bail* till the day of the trial. "Well, they always do that with people accused of a crime, don't they?" he asked.

"Not with dangerous criminals," Father said. "Remember, the cats are being held for murder . . . Now, Harry, would you have time enough to prepare your defense by Monday?"

"Sure. I've got the case pretty well solved already. But how about a jury?"

"Oh, there's a nice problem. We'll never be able to pick twelve unprejudiced jurors on the

Island: half the people don't like the Van Pelts, and the other half don't like cats. Could we do without a jury?"

"Of course not," Mother said. "I'm the Clerk. That's my job. Trust me to get a jury together by Monday — if I have to visit every house in town."

"But who will the judge be?" Mary asked.

"I know the very man for the job," Father said. "Andrew Carroll, the best criminal lawyer in Boston, came over on the boat with me today. He is planning to spend all next week in Nantucket. I'll go over to his place this evening and put the proposition up to him. I have an idea he'll snap at the chance to have a bit of innocent fun."

Mother, acting as Clerk, had got a pencil and paper and in the most businesslike manner was taking notes of the proceedings — setting down dates, names, facts. With a little help from Father she composed a form for the subpoenas which were to be served on the witnesses. Then the furniture was dragged around till the living room was made to look like a courtroom, as it would on Monday. The meeting was adjourned when Father left to go call on Mr. Carroll.

At bedtime the cats could not be found. It was then that Mother said, "I sometimes wonder what I was thinking of when I let you accept Beatrice. She's been a constant source of trouble. But this is the worst. I've had enough!"

"Mother, how can you say that?" Mary said. "She's the sweetest and brightest cat that ever lived."

"You forget, Mary, the things that aren't so sweet about her: how she has practically torn our best armchair to pieces, the number of times we've had to take her to the veterinarian for her itchy skin, the trouble we've had finding homes for her kittens — now this guinea-pig business . . . Why, at this very minute she and that good-for-nothing George are probably eating the second guinea pig!"

"But how did they get out?"

"How can they be kept in? Don't they find a way to get whatever they want? . . . But don't stand around doing nothing. Go out and hunt for them."

57

But the two cats were not found that night, either outdoors or indoors, though the five Reeds searched every square inch of the house and wandered around the neighborhood for an hour calling their names and making seductive noises. Paul feared they had gone down to the harbor and drowned themselves rather than submit to the shame of a trial, which caused Jennie to say it was a mistake to have talked about the trial in front of them.

The next morning the mystery was cleared up when Mother went to the linen closet to get some fresh dish towels and saw a pair of black ears sticking up above a pile of sheets. Beatrice, knowing that she was going to be forced into the ugly cellar that night, had slipped into the closet when the door was open for a minute, and bedded down with George in a snug corner, turning a deaf ear to all the calling and pleading. Even Mother, so angry with them the night before, had to admit that this was a very clever thing for an animal to do, and Beatrice was restored to favor in the Reed household.

5

THE NEXT DAY being Sunday, everybody went
to church. It was another beautiful morning,
and after the service people stood about in
little groups talking. Father and Mother
stopped to chat with Mr. and Mrs. Van Pelt;
and, as Paul said later, "They were so sweet that
butter wouldn't have melted in their mouths."
Not a word was said about the guinea pig.
Lydia and Alexandra, however, were not so
sweet, but stood apart and tossed their heads
and whispered to each other, making uncom-
plimentary remarks about Mary's hat and Jennie's dress. Not intimidated by her haughti-
ness, Harry walked over to Lydia, shook hands
with her, and asked if he might drop in to see
her in the afternoon. "I have something very
important to talk over with you," he said.

Lydia simply could not be cold to Harry and answered, "Alexandra and I will be most happy to see you whenever you wish to call."

When they got home Mr. Reed said, "The Van Pelts don't seem to be worrying about their guinea pig. I believe we're making far too much fuss over it."

"Don't be too sure," Mother said. "There was a bit of ice in Mrs. Van Pelt's voice, and she looked queer. I, for one, will be glad when this business is settled and forgotten."

"Did you notice the pretty dress Lydia had on?" Harry asked, and immediately wished he had bitten his tongue off before speaking. For Mary flared up. "Of course my dress couldn't compare with hers! You two made me sick . . . 'Can I drop in a minute this afternoon?' . . . 'Oh yes, we'll be happy to see you whenever you wish to call.' "

"Harry's in love with Lydia! Harry's in love with Lydia!" Jennie mocked.

"Shut up, will you!" Harry said, his face turning bright red. "You don't have to love a person to be polite, do you? I suppose you girls don't know anything about politeness. Be-

60

sides, you know how important it is for Lydia to come to the trial. Now, who's going to get her there if I don't."

So Harry went over to talk to Lydia after lunch. He found her alone in the living room. She said she was glad he had come, and asked him to sit down.

"This is really a sort of business call," Harry said. "Here's something I want to give to you," and he handed her the subpoena.

Lydia, of course, could not make head or tail of it, and Harry had to explain what it was all about. When she understood that once the document was in her hand she was obliged to attend the trial as a witness, she dropped it as if it had burned her fingers. "I'm not going to accept it," she cried.

"But you can't get out of it now. You took it, and you must keep it. That's what the law says."

"What law? Whose law? Who are you to make a law?"

"By the law of the land you are forced to obey."

"No, no, no! I won't go to your old trial."

61

"Listen, Lydia," Harry pleaded. "You understand how terrible we feel about your guinea pig. You should understand, too, how bad we feel about our cats being accused of eating it. We don't believe they did it, and we think we can prove they didn't. So we're going to try them for murder. If they're found guilty, they'll be punished; but, if they're acquitted, they'll go free. We must clear this up."

"Yes, and how will they be punished? They ought to be killed the way they killed my little pet."

"The punishment will depend on the Judge."

"And who will the Judge be? One of your family, I suppose, so they'll be sure of being acquitted."

Harry told her, "No, the Judge will be Mr. Carroll. He's one of the greatest criminal lawyers. Your father must know about him. He'll be absolutely just . . . Father's going to be the Prosecuting Attorney, and I'm going to represent the cats. You'll see, the whole trial will be honest and impartial . . . But you simply must appear as a witness. You're the prosecuting witness. Won't you come?"

Harry could see that Lydia was weakening. "Of course," she said, "if the trial is perfectly honest, the cats will be found guilty. Then you'll have to punish them."

"So you will come?"

"When and where will the trial be held?"

63

"In our living room, at two o'clock Monday."

"Nothing will ever make me believe the cats didn't eat my baby. Nobody else could have done it."

"That will be cleared up at the trial. Will you come?"

"I'll ask Mam-ma."

Harry went home feeling that Lydia was getting into the spirit of the game, and that even if her mother objected, she would find means to overcome her objection. Lydia's tears, he knew, flowed at the slightest hint of grief.

While Harry was serving his subpoena Paul was out hunting bones. Saturday afternoon he had followed Mary's advice and gone to Jake Salt's place while the old man was down at the wharf. He had searched for more than an hour on every side of the little house, going all the way across the lot to the next street, but without finding a single fresh bone, though there were many old chicken and rabbit bones lying about. So Paul had concluded that the guinea pig had not yet been eaten, but was being kept for Sunday dinner.

64

The next afternoon he stood watch, and as soon as he saw Mr. Salt, dressed in what he called his Sunday clothes, lock his door and go down toward the pier, he returned to the search. This time he had better luck. At a short distance from the back door he came across a handful of small bones so fresh that tiny scraps of meat were still on them. These had certainly not been there the day before. Paul got down on his hands and knees and picked up the valuable pieces of evidence and dropped them into the paper bag he had brought with him. While he was looking around for more, a shadow fell across the grass in front of him. He looked up — and there stood Jake Salt!

"Wa-al, young man, what are you doin' in my back yard?" he asked threateningly.

Paul sat back on his heels frightened half to death. Luckily for him, he had an answer ready. "I'm gathering mushrooms, Sir," he said.

"Toadstools, eh? . . . Ain't goin' to find none here."

"I didn't . . . didn't know. You see, mush-

rooms come up thick after a rain — specially in August. We like mushrooms at our house."

The old man's sharp eyes bored through and through the stammering boy. Then he looked meaningfully at the paper bag shaking in his hand, and for a minute Paul thought he was going to ask to see what was in it.

"Ain't no toadstool here," he said finally. "And ain't never been none. Guess you'd better be gettin' home, boy; and don't never come back. I don't like folks prowlin' around my house."

Paul, glad to get off so easily, jumped to his feet and hurried away without saying "Goodbye" or "Thank you." In his paper bag he carried the evidence which, he was sure, would prove the innocence of his cats. This was well worth the fright that had left him weak in the knees and a bit sick at the stomach.

6

Court convened at two o'clock sharp. The two Attorneys, the Clerk, the witnesses, and the jury were all in their places, when the Judge, wearing a black gown borrowed from the church organist, entered and took his place behind the table serving as the Bench.

The Clerk of the Court (Mother), following Mr. Carroll's order, had done her best to get twelve jurors together, but had been able to find only eight. These were seated along the wall at the right of the Bench. The two cats, imprisoned in an old lobster pot, had been carried in and placed on a stool in the center of the room. There was only one spectator, Alexandra Van Pelt, and she was seated beside Lydia with the other witnesses.

As the Judge walked into the room the Clerk

cried, "Please rise! . . . The Court!"

Everybody stood up, and the Clerk read in a singsong voice from a paper Mr. Carroll had given her: "Oyez, oyez, all persons having any manner of business before the honorable court of Nantucket County, draw nigh and give your attention, for the Court is now sitting . . . Be seated."

When they had all taken their seats again, sobered by the formal proceedings, the Clerk addressed the Judge, "Your Honor, we have before us the case of the State against the defendants, Beatrice and George Reed."

"Very well, Mrs. Clerk," said the Judge. "Please read the charges."

Then Mother read: "Beatrice and George Reed, you are hereby charged with having on or about Friday, August 22nd, eaten an animal commonly known as a Guinea pig, of the genus *Cavia*, belonging to the Misses Lydia and Alexandra Van Pelt." Then, facing the cats, "How do the defendants plead — guilty or not guilty?"

Beatrice, realizing that she was being spoken to, answered in her customary way by opening her mouth two or three times without making a sound. George rubbed his face against the slats of the cage to show his good intentions.

"Repeat the question, Mrs. Clerk," said the Judge. "I fear the defendants have not understood you."

"Do the defendants plead guilty or not guilty?" Mother repeated.

Harry got to his feet. "Your Honor," he said. "My clients wish to plead *not guilty*."

"Very well, Counselor," the Judge said. "Now, call the jury, Mrs. Clerk."

Mother read the names of the eight jurors. These were Mrs. Carroll, the two Carroll boys, the Carroll housemaid and gardener, Mr. Jones the grocer, Frank the postman, and Mrs. Bell Candle, the old lady who "tidied up" for the Reeds. The Carroll family had provided most of the jurors, for, of course, no one related to either the Van Pelts or the Reeds could be expected to be impartial.

The Judge then asked whether counsel for either side had any questions to put to the jurors. Under Father's questioning it became clear that the postman *disliked the Van Pelts;*

71

and Harry made Mrs. Bell Candle admit that she *disliked cats*. The good woman was sorry as soon as she said that, for she really wanted to be on the jury and have her part in hanging the two "pests." Both those jurors were rejected, though they were allowed to sit in the room as spectators.

The six remaining jurors then settled down to listen to the Prosecutor's opening address. Father outdid himself. "Ladies and gentlemen of the jury," he said. "Murder is always an ugly crime, but it seems to us that the murder with which the defendants are charged was particularly brutal and callous. The victims were the most inoffensive and defenseless animals in the world. The accused cannot plead hunger as a motive, for they are known to be pampered, overfed pets. If they committed this odious crime — and we hope to prove beyond a shadow of a doubt that they did commit it — then it must have been in a spirit of ruthless ferocity. We are convinced that, after listening to the evidence, you will declare them guilty. As intelligent a panel of jurors as you are cannot fail to bring in that verdict."

Then followed Harry's opening address, which was short and to the point. "Ladies and gentlemen of the jury, we are here to prove that the charges made by the counsel for the State are entirely false. We intend to show you that the defendants are innocent of the dreadful crime of murder. We will not take up any more of your time, but will proceed to establish their innocence. We know that you will pay close attention to the testimony and will not let yourselves be swayed and blinded to the true facts of the case by the brilliance of my colleague, the Prosecuting Attorney."

The Judge smiled behind his hand as Harry sat down. Then he said, "The Attorneys may now call their witnesses."

Lydia was the first witness called by the prosecution. The poor girl, ordinarily pale, was as white as a sheet and trembling all over. She could not have been more nervous if she herself had been on trial. After giving her name she swore *to tell the truth, the whole truth, and nothing but the truth,* and sat down.

"Now Miss Van Pelt," Father began kindly. "Will you tell the Court exactly what took place on the afternoon of Friday, August 22nd? Take your time, and have no fear: you are among friends."

"Well, it was raining . . . and we didn't go out to play . . . but about four o'clock I put on my raincoat and went out to take our guinea pigs their supper . . . And then . . . then . . ." Lydia choked up and stopped.

"Yes, what did you find when you went out with their food?"

"The door of the cage was open, and one o. the poor little things was gone!"

"You had a pair? Where was the other?"

"All hunched up at the back of the cage — looking scared."

"And what made you suspect the neighbors' cats?"

"Earlier that same afternoon Mam-ma looked out of the window and saw the two awful cats sitting on top of the cage, running their paws down through the wire, trying to get at the poor dears."

"Yes . . . Now, did those cats often come around the cage?"

"All the time . . . We had to drive them

74

away every day. We always said that one day the nasty animals would eat them."

Harry jumped to his feet. "I object, your Honor," he said. "The witness is expressing an opinion."

"Objection sustained," said the Judge. "The Clerk will strike out that part of the witness's testimony . . . Proceed, Counselor."

"Had you heard or seen anybody, or anything else near the cage that afternoon?"

"No, sir."

"And you have no reason to suspect anybody or anything else of taking the guinea pig?"

"No, sir. Everybody loved them — all but those awful cats."

"Your Honor," concluded the Prosecutor, "I have no further questions to ask this witness."

"Does Counsel for the Defense have any questions?" asked the Judge.

Harry rose for the cross-examination. "Miss Van Pelt," he said, in a voice he tried hard to keep on a bass level. "I understand you did not actually *see* the accused take your guinea pig. Am I right?"

"Yes, you are right; but that doesn't prove they didn't . . . Nobody else but them . . ."

The Judge rapped with his gavel. "Witness will kindly confine herself to answering the questions," he said.

Lydia flushed and looked uncomfortable.

"Now, Miss Van Pelt," Harry went on. "I want you to describe for the Court the lock on the door of the guinea-pig cage."

"Well, there's a big staple on the frame, with an iron band with a slit in it that slips down over the staple, and a wooden peg that runs down through the staple."

Harry stepped to the bench holding a piece of paper. "Your Honor," he said. "I should like to take the liberty of showing you a drawing I have made of that lock. I fear that the witness's description is not clear."

The Judge examined the drawing, then, "Proceed, Counselor," he said gravely.

Harry went on with his questioning. "And that lock is adequate to keep the door closed?"

"It always has. It never came open before."

"Now, was the door left open Saturday afternoon so the guinea pig could get out itself?"

76

"Oh, no!"

"How can you be so sure?"

"I shut it myself. I remember that after I gave the babies their lunch I fastened the door carefully. I am sure of that."

"And no one could have gone out, or got in

the garden and opened the door, between the time you fed the animals at noon and four o'clock, when you found one of them gone?"

"No, nobody."

"Yet somebody *could* have come into the garden from the street without being seen from the house?"

"Somebody could have . . . but nobody did."

"Was your mother or one of you looking out of the window all afternoon?"

"Not all the time, but Mam-ma saw the cats playing on the cage."

"Still, you admit it was possible for somebody or something to get at the cage without being seen?"

In a low voice Lydia answered, "Yes."

"Now, Miss Van Pelt, do you recall a conversation you had with me the morning after the crime?"

"Of course I do. Why should I forget it?"

"Then you recall that after looking at the lock, we both agreed it would be next to impossible for a cat to open it when the peg was pushed down tight?"

"*You* said it would be: I didn't. I said, 'Cats can open anything.'"

"Your Honor, if you will allow this witness to step down, I should like to put a person on the stand who will testify to the possibility of a cat opening that door." As neither the Judge nor the Prosecutor had any objections, Paul was sworn and took his seat in the witness box.

"Mr. Reed," Harry began. "I understand you are an expert in the matter of locks?"

"I am, sir."

"You have the reputation of being able to open all kinds of locks, bolts, and so forth. And you can take apart and put together any lock made. Is that correct?"

"I guess it is."

"Did you examine the lock on the guinea-pig cage shortly after the disappearance of the victim?"

"I did."

"And will you tell the Court exactly what you found?"

"Well, the cage was shut . . . just as the last witness said, with a strong wood peg run down through a staple."

"In your opinion — and you are an expert — could a cat have lifted the peg out of the staple?"

"No, sir, it couldn't. It was a man did that."

The Prosecutor jumped to his feet. "I object, your Honor! This calls for a conclusion. The witness's testimony on this point is entirely irrelevant."

"Objection sustained," said the Judge. "The witness will merely answer the questions."

"I have no more questions, your Honor," Harry said. "I am through with this witness."

But the prosecution was not through with Paul. Father took his stand in front of the fidgeting boy, and leveling his forefinger at him, shouted: "Will you tell the Court how you acquired your reputation as a lock expert?"

Paul grew pink and stammered, "Whv — why — in lots of ways."

"For example?"

"Well, once when I was shut up in my room I managed to pick the lock from the inside. Another time I slid a bolt on the kitchen door of a house locked up for the winter."

"Yes . . . go on."

"And once I picked the lock on your fishing-
tackle box. And I did repair Mother's brace-
let."

"Your Honor," Father said with deepest
scorn. "I submit that this witness is a fraud,
and that his testimony proves nothing — ex-
cept his own criminal nature. His findings,

81

therefore, cannot be accepted as trustworthy. I am — through with him!"

"You may stand down, young man," the Judge said coldly, and Paul crept back to his seat between Mary and Jennie.

"Now," said the Judge, rising. "If the counselors have no objection, I shall declare a recess of one hour, in which time we will all have a cup of tea. The jurors may remain here and have some refreshments, but I must warn them against speaking to any person in the room. Court recessed till four o'clock."

The jurors were the only ones who enjoyed the wonderful refreshments Mother had laid out in the dining room. There were cakes, piles of sandwiches, tea, lemonade. Those goodies would ordinarily have disappeared at the Reeds' like a snowfall in July, but today almost everybody was too upset to eat. Lydia and Alexandra politely refused everything that was offered to them, Mary and Jennie were trying to comfort the prisoners by pushing scraps of a tuna sandwich through the bars of their cage, Harry was scolding his last witness.

"You were my best hope," he grumbled.

"But you goofed and got all balled up, and didn't prove anything."

"I swear I couldn't help it!" Paul whined. "Father just scared the wits out of me."

"Well, watch out when I call you the next time to testify about Jake Salt. Don't let Father make you say anything foolish."

Little Mrs. Bell Candle was having a wonderful time, wandering around and around the plates, cups and bowls on the table; and when she had eaten her fill she stuffed a good supply of the less perishable sandwiches and cookies into her old black handbag.

On the whole the recess was an unpleasant period, with people divided into clans and not speaking to each other, so that the Judge sighed with relief when the clock struck four and he could reconvene the court.

7

THE PROSECUTOR called Mother to the stand. There was a naughty gleam in his eye as he began. "Mrs. Reed, how long have you known the accused?"

"I have known Beatrice, the mother cat, since she was brought into our house two years ago. I have known her son George since he was born, eight weeks ago."

"Yes . . . Now, have you ever seen them catch and devour any small animal or bird?"

"Naturally. All cats do."

"What kind of animals?"

"Oh, nearly all kinds. Especially mice — and birds, and once a young rabbit."

"You did see the mother eat a woodchuck once?"

"Yes . . . isn't she a cat?"

"Then, in your opinion the defendants could have eaten a guinea pig?"

"Objection!" shouted Harry. "That calls for a conclusion."

"Objection overruled," said the Judge. "I believe that this witness is in a position to make such a conclusion. Proceed."

"I will repeat my question. Mrs. Reed, in your opinion could the defendants have eaten the guinea pig?"

Mother was facing the lobster pot, and at that moment Beatrice yawned and half closed her eyes as if insolently winking at her. She hesitated.

"Come, come, madam, you must not let your sympathy for the accused influence you. Answer my question."

"Yes," Mother whispered. "I believe they could very well have eaten the poor animal."

"Thank you. Now that we have established that point, will you tell the Court whether you have found the accused cruel in their treatment of smaller animals?"

"Why, I suppose you could call it that, though . . ."

"Just answer the questions, please," the Judge ordered.

"Yes, they acted cruelly at times."

"Aha! . . . They took delight in tormenting their prey, and had no pity on their struggles and screams?"

"None . . . *But they are cats!*"

"Yes, I think no one could doubt that . . . The witness is yours, Counselor."

Harry rose to cross-question Mother. He adopted an entirely new line of questioning. "Mrs. Reed, do the prisoners have good appetites?"

"Indeed they do. I suppose you could say they like to eat."

"But do they eat when they aren't hungry?"

"Of course not. You couldn't make them touch a mouthful when they don't want it."

"What time were they fed on the day of the crime?"

"Let me see . . . At noon, as usual, then again about six o'clock."

"Now I want you to think carefully before answering my next question. *Were they hungry at supper time?*"

"Yes, they were, very hungry. I remember
clearly, for that day we had clam chowder for
supper, something they love."

"Did they eat as if they were hungry?"

"They didn't leave a scrap."

"Good! Now I want you to tell the Court
whether in your opinion the cats would have
eaten their supper *if they had devoured a
whole guinea pig two hours earlier?*"

"Objection!" shouted Father. "This calls
for a conclusion which the witness is not in a
position to give, not being a cat herself and
never having felt cat-hunger."

"Objection overruled," said the Judge. "It

seems to me it is most relevant. Answer the question, madam."

"I certainly do not believe Beatrice and George would have eaten any supper if they had already had a good meal of guinea pig," Mother said emphatically.

"Thank you, Mrs. Reed," Counsel said smugly. "I have no further question, your Honor." When Mother stepped down everybody felt that Defense had scored a point, and things were looking a trifle brighter for the prisoners.

Mary was the next to take the stand. She looked so distressed that the Judge felt called upon to say a few words of comfort to her. Then Father put his first question: "You were at home on Friday, August 22?"

"Yes, sir, I was."

"And you were a witness of all the tragic proceedings that have been described to the Court?"

"Yes, I was."

"What was done with the accused that evening when the family retired?"

"They were shut up in the cellar."

"Tell the Court why."

"For fear they might get at the other guinea pig."

"Aha! . . . Then you admit you thought the cats might be guilty?"

"Yes, we thought they could have done it."

"Good . . . Were they still in the cellar the next morning when you came down to breakfast?"

"No. Jennie had let them out."

"So you went outside to look for the cats?"

"Yes."

"And when you found them, what were they doing?"

Mary realized she was trapped, and looked appealingly around the room. "Answer my question, please," said the Prosecutor.

"The two cats were eating . . . pulling at something."

"And what was that *something?*"

"It was . . . a . . . guinea-pig skin."

Lydia, who had up to then been ignorant of this aspect of the case, looked grimly at Harry.

"So they were eating a guinea-pig skin?"

"I didn't mean they were eating it. They were just pulling at it."

"As you will . . . Would you recognize that object if you saw it again?"

"I suppose I would."

"Your Honor," Father said. "I would like to introduce Exhibit 1 at this point," and he unrolled a flat package and held up the skin which had been thawing out since early morning. "Now, Miss Reed, is this the skin they were chewing?"

"I guess it is."

"We want you to be sure. Is this that skin?"

"Yes."

"That is all . . . Your Honor, I should like to recall a previous witness."

"You may stand down, Miss Reed," said the Judge. "Counsel, call your witness."

"Will Miss Lydia Van Pelt please take the stand," Father said. "Now, Miss Van Pelt, will you kindly examine this exhibit and tell the Court if you recognize it."

"Indeed I do."

"And what is it?"

90

"It is our poor dear black-and-white guinea pig's skin," Lydia cried, bursting into tears.

"I understand that the sight of this object causes you great distress," Father said kindly, "and I will not trouble you with any further questions."

"But I will," Harry said roughly, coming forward and picking up the skin. "Now, Miss Van Pelt I must ask you to examine this piece of evidence most carefully . . . Take this pencil and spread it out . . . Look it over . . . Tell the Court, is it torn and shredded as it certainly would have been if two sharp-toothed animals — like cats — had been tearing at it?"

"Why, no . . . it's whole."

"Thank you . . . Now, your Honor, I should like to be allowed to show this exhibit to the jury."

"Request granted," said the Judge.

Harry laid the skin in front of Mr. Jones the grocer, and spread it out carefully with the aid of two pencils. "You can see that this skin has not been chewed, torn, or in any way mutilated," he said.

"By jove!" said Mr. Jones.

"And you can also see," Harry went on, "that the carcass could not have been eaten by cats without destroying the skin."

One after another the jurors moved forward to examine the exhibit. They took so long about it that the Judge rapped with his gavel and said sharply, "Time is passing, Counselor. Proceed."

"I have no further question to put to this witness, your Honor," Harry said, and sat down. Over in the lobster pot George was working at the fastening of the door, mewing plaintively. Beatrice had fallen asleep. Lydia, back in her seat, put her arms around her little sister and tenderly wiped a tear from her pale cheek — a sight to move the heart of the sternest juror.

"Has Counsel for the State any further witnesses to examine?" asked the Judge.

"I have not, your Honor. I am satisfied that we have already established the guilt of the prisoners."

"And Counsel for the Defense?"

"I have two, your Honor," Harry said. "I should like to recall a previous witness — Mr. Paul Reed."

"Will Mr. Paul Reed kindly take the stand?"

Paul stepped forward holding a small tin box in his hand. When he was seated Harry took the box from him and held it up so that everybody could see it.

"Your Honor," he said. "I should like this object marked Exhibit 2."

"The Clerk will so mark it for identification," ordered the Judge.

"I intend to prove that this box contains — guinea-pig bones." Harry continued in an emphatic voice.

A surprised whisper ran around the room. "Order in the court!" cried the Judge. "If there is any further disturbance of this nature, I shall have to clear the room . . . Proceed with your questioning, Counselor."

"Now, Mr. Reed," Harry went on. "Will you tell the Court where you found the bones contained in this box."

"In a lot back of a house I do not care to mention."

94

"Yes . . . that you dare not mention for fear of incriminating a person who is not on trial for this crime . . . You will, therefore, refrain from giving any clue that might establish this person's identity . . . When did you find the bones?"

"Yesterday afternoon."

"Had you looked for them earlier?"

"Yes I had . . . Saturday afternoon. The day after the guinea pig disappeared."

"And you didn't find anything then?"

"No. So I thought he hadn't eaten the guinea pig yet."

"But yesterday you went back and looked again. And did you find anything?"

"I picked up the bones in that box."

"And what kind of bones are they?"

"Guinea-pig bones, of course."

"Thank you . . . Your Honor, I have no further questions."

"May I examine the evidence?" the Judge asked. The Clerk passed the box up to him; he took off the lid and peered in. "Hmm!" he muttered. "Looks like the leftovers from somebody's picnic! . . . Thank you . . . Would

95

the Prosecutor care to cross-examine this witness?"

"I certainly would," Father said, stepping forward. "Now, young man, would you tell the jury just why you looked in that particular back yard for bones?"

Paul squirmed. "Well . . . well . . . we thought everything pointed toward that man — that person. He said he liked guinea pig."

"I see. In short, you acted on a hunch."

"I guess so, sir."

"And you might just as well have suspected anybody else — his Honor the Judge, for instance — and gone and rooted around in his back yard for bones?"

"No, not anybody else. This person had reasons for killing the guinea pig."

"So you actually picked this poor person out of all the inhabitants of the Island, and pinned the crime on him?"

"We had reasons."

"Purely circumstantial." Then Father put his finger close to Paul's face and shouted. "Can't you see that your conduct was despicable? How dared you go and look around the

96

place of a person whose name had not even been mentioned in connection with this case? Did you want to send an innocent man to the gallows?"

Paul slumped down in his chair and said nothing. "Answer my question, sir," Father roared.

"No, no . . . we didn't."

"Aha! . . . And you claim that these things in your miserable box are guinea-pig bones. How do you know?"

"Why, they couldn't be anything else."

"So you are a biologist as well as a locksmith! Did you ever see a guinea-pig skeleton?"

"No, sir."

"You acted on another hunch in bringing those bones into court today. You could have picked up any old bones, in my yard or his Honor's yard, and claimed they were guinea-pig bones."

"But these aren't old bones. They weren't there Saturday."

"Your Honor, this witness is entirely untrustworthy. I suggest that your Honor disregard his testimony."

"That's my business," the Judge said dryly. "You may stand down, young man."

Paul ran back to his seat like a mouse let out of a trap, and sat down with a face so red a match could have been lit on it. Harry, feeling flattened out and beaten, called Mother to the stand.

"Will you please examine these bones, Mrs. Reed," he said, "and tell the Court what you think of them?"

Mother took the bones in her hand one after another and looked at them carefully. "They are the bones of some small animal, like a squirrel or rat."

"Could they be rabbit bones?"

"No, they are too small."

"Nor chicken bones?"

"Not possibly. This animal had ribs and vertebrae."

"You are familiar with the various small animals used as food?"

"I should be by this time."

"Is a guinea pig an eatable animal?"

"I understand that some people eat them."

"Could these be the bones of a guinea pig?"

"They very well could be. I believe they are."

"In your opinion are these old dry bones?"

"No. They look as fresh as if they had just been cleaned."

"Not earlier than Friday or Saturday?"

"That is my opinion."

"Thank you . . . I have no further questions to put to this witness, your Honor."

Then the Prosecutor tackled the witness; and before he was through, the last shred of Harry's confidence had deserted him.

"Mrs. Reed," Father began. "Have you ever eaten a guinea pig?"

"Of course not."

"Do you know any one who has?"

"Not that I can think of offhand."

"Then you've never seen guinea-pig bones?"

"Frankly, I have not."

"Strange, then, that you could be so sure of the exact nature of this exhibit. *Are* you sure? Remember, you are under oath."

"Well, while I wouldn't swear they are guinea-pig bones, I do feel that they are very much like — what guinea-pig bones must — be like."

"Your sentence is a bit confused, yet I believe I understand your meaning . . . Have you ever seen the bones of a prairie dog?"

"Never. Why do you ask?"

100

"Or of a ferret, or a weasel, or a marmot, or a duckbill platypus?"

"Of course not!" Mother exclaimed. "But there's no reason to make a fool of me."

"My dear Mrs. Reed," Prosecutor said solemnly. "It was far from our thought to do anything of the sort. Besides, one is what one is. Nobody can change that."

"Your Honor, I object to this! Counsel has stopped questioning and gone to insulting!" Mother cried. A muttering and scuffling was heard in the courtroom. "Silence!" roared the Judge, bringing down his gavel. "Proceed, Counselor."

"Now, Mrs. Reed, I want you to answer me simply: are the specimens in this box guinea-pig bones?"

"Oh, I don't know . . . I don't know anything now!" Mother said.

"That is all, your Honor," Father said. "I am quite satisfied."

"The witness may step down," said the Judge, a mean little twinkle in his eye. "Has Counsel for the Defense any other witnesses?"

"I have not, your Honor," Harry said hopelessly.

The Judge stood up, hiding a yawn behind his hand. "The Bench wishes to retire to his chambers to study the testimony that has been laid before him," he said. "Court is recessed for ten minutes."

Everybody relaxed a little in the absence of the Judge. Father had evidently made himself unpopular with the faction that wanted the cats cleared. They all avoided him, but cast accusing glances in his direction as they whispered among themselves.

Mary said, "Father intends to hang the poor things."

And Paul said, "I'll never speak to him again if he does."

Lydia and Alexandra, on the contrary, were very sweet to him. "You did a wonderful job, Mr. Reed," Lydia said. "You showed them up. Alexandra and I want to thank you."

Father smiled. "Look at him," Harry said bitterly. "Eating up the compliments of those two sillies!"

"I know one thing," Mary said. "You're going to need all your eloquence for your closing speech. I have an idea the Prosecutor is going to lay it on pretty thick. It's up to you now."

Mr. Carroll returned at that moment, looking as serious as a judge — as the saying goes. The smell of tobacco that came into the room with him gave a clue to the reason for the recess.

"Court reconvened," he said pompously. "We will now hear the summation of the prosecution."

Harry stood up. "Your Honor," he said. "I should like to call one last witness. I am aware that this is unusual, but I feel that there is one point that has not been proved. I should like to call Miss Jennie Reed to the stand."

"Request granted," said the Judge. "Will Miss Jennie Reed take the stand."

After the formality of name-giving, swearing and so forth, Harry began: "Now, Miss Reed, would you tell the Court how well you know the prisoners?"

"Awful well . . . I'm Beatrice's mother and George's grandmother."

"Exactly what do you mean by that?"

"I mean, I take care of them more than anybody else. They're my kitties . . . I feed them."

"When she doesn't forget them," Paul whispered to Mary.

"Then, Miss Reed, you would say you really know them?"

"Indeed I do. I ought to."

"Would you say they are cruel, as a previous

witness has tried to establish, or kind and gentle?"

"Oh, they're not cruel. They never scratch or bite or spit at me, and Beatrice lets me turn her over on her back and clean her eyes."

"You wouldn't say they are cruel with other animals?"

"Of course not."

"You don't believe they'd eat a guinea pig?"

"Oh dear, no. They love the guinea pigs. They always want to go over and play with them."

"Thank you, Miss Reed . . . I have no more questions, your Honor."

"Perhaps the Prosecutor would like to cross-examine the witness," said the Judge.

Father half stood up, then looked at the flushed, trembling little girl, and sat down again. "No questions, your Honor," he said gently.

"Then the witness may step down," the Judge said. "Now we are ready to listen to the argument of Counsel for the Prosecution."

105

8

FATHER cleared his throat, threw out his chest, and began. "Ladies and gentlemen of the jury, I ask you to take a careful look at the prisoners who here stand charged with a heinous crime. I strongly advise you not to let yourselves be deceived by appearances; for certainly no creature ever looked gentler, less rapacious than they." He paused for a moment while all eyes studied the inmates of the lobster pot, now both peacefully sleeping, then he went on: "Inside those pretty mouths are rows of cruelly sharp teeth, and hidden within those velvet paws are needlelike claws, ready to spring out at the slightest provocation. It is well known that the cat is the most hypocritical of animals. A hypocrite, your Honor, is a creature that conceals its true nature behind a mask. Now, the cruelest of natures lurks behind the cat's mask of innocence, gentleness, and affection. Who has not seen one of those beasts, deaf to the pitiful cries of its victim, tear a songbird to shreds? What person has not been rewarded for his or her patient care and generous love by a hateful bite or scratch? Ah, trust them not — those prisoners so touchingly asleep in their cage; for they are capable of the most atrocious crimes.

"In my opening speech I suggested that there are various degrees of ugliness in the crime of murder. It seems to me that the crime we are judging today is the ugliest of the ugly. Consider the victim: a soft little animal that nature failed to provide with adequate means of defense or protection. No long sharp teeth, no powerful limbs, no strong claws. Under certain conditions it might be able to run fast enough to escape from an enemy; but this means of escape was denied our poor victim, as it was confined in a small cage. Run about in terror as it would, it could not get beyond the reach of the wicked thieving claws.

"Consider the circumstances. It is a raw,

rainy day. The garden in which the cage is kept is deserted. No friendly ear is near to hear a despairing cry, no friendly hand is near to offer help. A pair of cats creep up, leap on top of the cage, and begin to work at the peg which keeps the door shut. Imagine the terror of the imprisoned animals as they look up and see four glowing yellow eyes staring at them! So frightened are they that they are struck powerless: all they can do is cower in a corner. The cats continue their dastardly work — lifting, pulling, twisting, till finally the peg is released and the door swings open. Then the snarling, spitting beasts fall on the defenseless victim and drag him forth to devour him. And no one sees the crime or hears the last agonized shriek!"

At this point in the Prosecutor's speech a gasp was heard, then a voice crying, "Look at Lydia! Oh, look at Lydia!" Everybody did look at Lydia and saw that she had fallen over and was lying white and still against her little sister. Mother hurried to her and began slapping her hands and cheeks. Paul rushed out of the room and was back in an instant carrying a

glass of ice water, which he would have poured
over her head if Mary had not caught his hand.
In a minute the girl moved, moaned, opened
her eyes and sat up. "Oh, it was so beautiful!"
she gasped. "So very beautiful!"

"Thank goodness you're better!" Mother
said. "You gave us a terrible fright . . . How
do you feel now? Do you think you should sit
through the rest of the trial, or would you
rather go home?"

"Oh, I want to stay. I feel all right — really I do. Mr. Reed's speech just broke my heart. But it was so true. I'm all right. Go on, please."

"Take it easy, Dad," Harry whispered to his father, and the Judge advised, "Do not let your feelings get the better of you, Counsel. Try to fit your language to the ears of the young . . . Proceed."

And father went on with his speech, looking sheepish and making far less noise. "My honored opponent," with a wave of his hand at Harry, "has tried to show that the accused could not lift the wooden peg which kept the door of the cage closed. It would seem logical that cats could not do this; but cats escape all logic. There is nothing in the world some cat cannot do, from swimming the ocean to climbing the Empire State Building. Give certain cats time enough, and they would pick the lock of the town bank. Maybe some cats could not have pulled that peg out; but our cats could, and did. I trust, gentlemen of the jury, that Counsel for the Defense has not convinced you they could not.

110

"Furthermore, the defense claims that the accused could not have eaten their supper that day if they had already devoured a guinea pig. This is laughable, your Honor. There is nothing impossible where cats' eating habits are concerned. While they can go for days without food, at other times they will eat without stopping from daylight to dark. They will eat flesh, fish, fruit, vegetables, bread, cake, pie, candy, eggs — whatever they find. Give them a big supper and they will polish off a couple of birds, a rabbit, and fifty crickets for dessert. I grant you that it does not seem likely that the accused would eat their supper on top of a whole guinea pig, but there is nothing in the rules that says they *could not do it.*

"Now we come to the matter of Exhibits 1 and 2 which Defense has presented as conclusive evidence of the innocence of his clients. Your Honor can clearly see that if we accept these pieces of evidence, the burden of guilt is lifted from the prisoners and placed on some person or persons unknown. But, your Honor, no such person has been named. It is the cats that are on trial, not some unnamed third per-

111

son. To imply that some human being did away with the victim is to cast doubt on some innocent man or woman in our neighborhood. This cannot be done. We shall probably never know what caused the witness for the defense — Private Eye Number 1 — to look for bones on the property of an honored citizen of our fair city. We can only pity his evil mind.

"Moreover, it would be ridiculous to admit that these are guinea-pig bones . . . On whose evidence, I ask you? The word of an ignorant schoolboy who couldn't tell an otter from a pig, and a simple housewife whose knowledge of anatomy doesn't go beyond the chain-store meat counter. Has Counsel for the Defense called an accredited biologist or naturalist to testify? If he had, we should bow before his superior knowledge; but we cannot form any true opinion of the nature of these exhibits on the testimony of such incompetent witnesses as have been called.

"The jury, then, has no choice but to find the accused guilty of murder in the first degree — cold, premeditated murder, without a single extenuating factor. We do, however, recommend that you show mercy to the younger of the criminals, on account of his youth and previous good record. We feel that he was led into crime by his mother, and recommend that the Court give him a light sentence. But for that depraved, unnatural mother we ask the maximum and extreme penalty — DEATH!"

When the Prosecutor sat down, mopping his forehead, Lydia and Alexandra clapped their hands loudly, which made the Judge frown and bring down his gavel with a bang.

Then Harry stood up for his closing speech. He was slow getting under way. Father had swept away the best of his arguments by making it impossible to introduce the skin and bones. All the other bits of evidence he had gathered in favor of the poor cats now seemed weak. For two or three minutes he floundered, getting nowhere, his wretched voice jumping wildly about from bass to soprano. Then suddenly he stiffened.

He had looked toward the lobster pot and seen Beatrice, her foot planted firmly on George's neck to keep him still, lovingly washing his little black-and-white face. Sensing the danger, she had turned on all her charm: her defender could do no less. Father's last word — DEATH — ringing in his ears, he threw back his shoulders and began.

"Ladies and gentlemen of the jury, you have been asked by the prosecutor to dismiss our strongest evidence as ir-re-lev-ant. He has tried to brush off lightly every fact we have carefully proved in favor of our clients. But we cannot allow that. We are not trying to put the blame on any third person. We have no interest in who else or what else might have taken the guinea pig. We just want to prove that it was impossible for our clients to take it. If the guilt must fall on somebody else, we are sorry.

"The fact remains that the skin was not messed up; and the accused could not have eaten the carcass without tearing the skin to pieces, or eating it along with the rest. Common sense tells us that . . . As for the peg on the door — it might be possible for certain cats to remove it; but it is not *likely* that our cats did it. And today we are interested in what is *likely,* not in the freakish and unusual . . . Then again, it might be possible for cats to eat a full meal with a whole guinea pig in their stomachs, but it is not *likely* that they would.

"Now we come to the question of the bones found by our witness in the field back of a nameless person's home. Father — eh — the Prosecutor says that should not be brought in. It can't be left out. Everybody agrees that those bones are not those of any animal we generally eat — cow, goat, sheep, fish, rabbit, chicken, pig. They were not in the field Saturday, but were suddenly there Sunday. Maybe there's no proof what they are; but it's far more likely they are guinea-pig bones than otter or weasel bones. We don't have marmots around here, and as far as I know no duckbill platypus is missing on the Island! It could be a rat, but nobody licks rat bones clean before throwing them out.

"I ask the jury to look at the accused." (Beatrice was still washing her son's face.) "Isn't that a beautiful picture of motherly love? Do you wonder that the pair have worked their way into the hearts of the Reed family? . . . Yet we are not going to make our appeal on the ground of sentiment. We are ready to grant

115

that the accused are neither better nor worse than other cats. We will grant that, being what they are, they do eat smaller animals. We will even grant that Beatrice's love for her kitten might have tempted her to catch a convenient guinea pig for his supper. But we argue that she *could* not have done that. We have produced evidence to show that it was physically impossible for the accused to get the guinea pig. We are not arguing that the accused *might not* have committed the crime: we are arguing that they *could* not.

"We therefore ask you, members of the Jury, to bring in a verdict of not guilty, and to set the wrongly accused animals free."

Harry sat down perspiring and red. With the exception of the Van Pelt girls and Mrs. Bell Candle, the courtroom burst into applause, and it was minutes before the Judge could restore order.

Then he rose and said, "I shall not make the customary charge to the jury, as I feel that all the facts have been clearly brought before you. If you are convinced, after listening to all the

116

testimony, that the defendants did willfully eat the guinea pig, you will declare them guilty. But if there is any doubt in your minds as to their guilt, you will acquit them. You will retire, if you please, and consider your verdict . . . Mrs. Clerk, will you accompany the jurors to a side room where they may deliberate."

As soon as the jury had filed out of the room, Father hurried over to Harry and shook his hand warmly. "I'm proud of you, son," he said. "I'm sure you've cleared the poor cats."

The tone of Father's voice and his friendly handclasp wiped out Harry's hurt, but Mary said bitterly, "No thanks to you, Dad, if he has cleared them."

"Come now," Father said. "You can certainly understand that I had to be a bit rough with you all. We didn't want the whole thing to look like a put-up job, did we? Would it have been quite honest if I had not opposed the Defense with all my might? Now Lydia can be sure — whatever the verdict may be — that the cats were tried fairly. She will have nothing to complain about."

Mother kissed Father, Jennie ran her hand into his, and Harry said, "No hard feelings, Dad. You were simply great."

At that moment the jurors came back into the room and took their seats. They had been out only a matter of minutes. They were all smiling, as if they had just heard a piece of good news.

"Have you reached a verdict?" the Judge asked solemnly.

"We have, your Honor," answered Mrs. Carroll who had been chosen as foreman.

"And what is your verdict?"

Mrs. Carroll's voice rang out clear and strong. "Not guilty, your Honor."

A sigh of relief ran through the room. Even the Judge seemed pleased. "In that case," he said, "I have only to order the prisoners to be released — immediately."

As Mary and Paul jumped up to open the lobster pot, the Judge added, "Just a minute, please. I have a final word to say. It is the Court's hope that this unfortunate incident will be soon forgotten and no hard feelings will live on to mar the friendly relations between you young people. Much as we might love our pets, no cat or guinea pig is worth the loss of friendship. May I advise the Reeds, though, that it would be wise for them to keep close watch over their cats; for one day they might — they just might . . . Court dismissed."

In a minute Beatrice was purring in Mary's arms, George in Paul's. Everybody was congratulating the counselors and thanking Mr. Carroll for acting as Judge. While he was getting out of his hot black gown, Mother told Mrs. Carroll, "Your husband makes a wonderful judge. He would grace any bench in the land. Tell him how much we admired him."

And Mrs. Carroll answered, "Your own boy Harry is a wonder. I shall look for him, if I live long enough, to rise to be Chief Justice of the Supreme Court."

As it was suppertime, the party broke up without delay. They all walked out on the terrace with the Carrolls. From that high point they looked down on the clustered houses and the blue-black sea glowing under the slanting rays of the late-summer sun.

"A great little town," Mr. Carroll said, draw-

119

ing a deep breath of the spicy air. "And didn't we have a wonderful afternoon! Where are the cats?"

They were brought over to him, and he solemnly shook Beatrice's paw and laid his hand as in a blessing on George's head. "Glad you got off without a punishment," he said.

In the excitement nobody noticed that Harry had gone over and stood by Lydia's side. "Would you like to go to the early show with me tomorrow?" he asked. "They say the picture is an awfully good one."

And Lydia answered, "I'll have to ask Mamma."

The next morning Father went over to Jake Salt's to get bait for the fishing trip he and the boys had planned. He walked along slapping his pant leg with a switch and whistling, so as to look natural. He found the old man sitting in his doorway mending a crab net.

"Nice morning, Mr. Salt," Father said cheerfully. "A welcome change after so much rain."

"Ay-eh," Salt answered without looking up.

"How's fishing these days?"

"Some mackerel runnin'."

"That's what I thought. I'd be satisfied to get a few of them."

"You want some bait, I reckon."

"That's what I came for. I'd like enough for four."

Salt laid aside his work and went into his house. Father would have liked to follow him, for the dirt and disorder of the old man's cabin was much discussed among the visitors to the Island, but Salt slammed the door in his face. In a minute he reappeared carrying a tin can.

"That'll be fifty cents," he said.

After Father had paid for the bait he still lingered, fidgeting and clearing his throat. Jake Salt gave him a distrustful look. Suddenly Father smiled and said in a matter-of-fact tone, "Come, Mr. Salt, as man to man, tell me about the guinea pig."

The old man took his pipe out of his mouth and spat, his black eyes boring a hole in the visitor. "Don't know nothin' 'bout no guinea pig," he said.

"You know what I'm talking about. The Van Pelt girls have lost one of their guinea pigs. I guess you could tell me where it is, couldn't you?"

Jake Salt took a step toward Father, looking positively dangerous. "See here, mister!" he said. "Are you crazy, or somethin'?"

"Oh, come! You can tell me. It won't go any further."

"I said I don't know nothin' 'bout no guinea pig. If you're lookin' for one, you'd best go somewhere else. I don't want to hear no more 'bout it . . . Good mornin'."

"You needn't be afraid . . ."

"I said good mornin', mister!" and bang! went Jake Salt's house door. And that was that. Bang!

J. David Townsend

J. DAVID TOWNSEND was born in Cape May, New Jersey, and attended school there before going on to the University of Pennsylvania and the University of Grenoble in France. He became a minister and his very active career includes eleven years in a mission school for Berber boys in Algiers and sixteen years as a minister in Paris. He also taught in the American School in Paris and lived there one year under the German occupation.

Mr. Townsend's years abroad provided the inspiration for this, his first book for children. There were indeed two cats who were accused of eating a neighbor's guinea pig, only this took place in a tiny medieval town in the south of France, where the Townsends spent their summers.

Now retired, Mr. Townsend and his French wife live in Bel Air, Maryland.